# WHO LOVES YOU, BILLY?

Collins
RED
*STORYBOOK*

*Other Collins books by Bernard Ashley*
King Rat

*For younger readers*
Cleversticks
A Present for Paul

*Find out about Bernard Ashley and his books on*
www.bernardashley.cwc.net

# WHO LOVES YOU, BILLY?

## Bernard Ashley

## Illustrated by Philip Hopman

Collins

*An imprint of* HarperCollins*Publishers*

First published in Great Britain by Collins in 2000
Collins is an imprint of HarperCollins*Publishers* Ltd
77-85 Fulham Palace Road, Hammersmith, London W6 8JB

3 5 7 9 8 6 4 2

ISBN 0 00 675459 7

The HarperCollins website address is
www.**fire**and**water**.com

Text copyright © Bernard Ashley 2000
Illustrations copyright © Philip Hopman 2000

The author and illustrator assert the moral right to
be identified as author and illustrator of the work.

Printed and bound in Great Britain by
Omnia Books Limited,
Glasgow G64

# CHAPTER ONE

Billy Smith was on free meals, and he didn't care who knew it. He'd always been a 'free'. His dad had gone off and his mum was always saying what a struggle it was to make ends meet. "The ends of what?" he'd ask – but she didn't know either. Except, it was something to do with money – the not having much of it.

When the dinner register was called Billy wasn't one of those who went up and secretly didn't give in any money. He shouted "Free!" without leaving the comfort of his seat. It didn't bug him; it wasn't a sin, being poor, he wasn't ashamed of it. The meals tasted the same whether you paid for them or not. And you didn't have to sit in a different part of the canteen or anything like that – everyone was in together whether they paid for their meals, got them free or brought packed lunches.

In any case, Billy never hung about over his food like someone sitting in the window of Pizza Hut. Meals were there to be got down as fast as you could before you went outside. Dinner *play* was the thing, not the dinner. He could sometimes eat a first course and an afters before Declan had got the wrapping off his packet of sandwiches.

Packed lunch people *were* a bit like that. They sat over their lunchboxes as if what was in them wasn't food but treasure they kept pulling out.

"Aaaah! Corned beef sandwich!" As if it was a wallet stuffed with banknotes.

"Ooooh! Lovely! Yogurt!" As if it was a silver goblet filled with frankincense.

"Eeeeh! Top score! A mandarin!" As if it was a golden ball for a princess to play with.

Billy's mutton stew was mutton stew, and Banana Bonanza was hot and soggy banana slices in runny custard – nothing to *aaaah! ooooh!* or *eeeeh!* about. Three minutes for the first plate, one minute for the second, a quarter of a minute skidding between tables – and how long did a wipe of the mouth take? He was in and out of the canteen in under five minutes; which left nearly an hour for fun.

And at school Billy needed his bits of fun – because there wasn't a lot at home these days.

He lived with his mum in a council flat on the Cherry Tree Estate (which hadn't seen a cherry in fifty years). The flat was small, and if he didn't fancy what was on the telly, there wasn't much else to do. There wasn't *room* to do much else, and she wouldn't let him go out to play, not round there. If he jumped on his bed or bounced a ball on the door there'd soon be a thumping through one of the walls. And his mum was busy, busy, busy trying to make those ends of something meet.

For a while she served in a greengrocer's – before it was closed and turned into a charity shop. Then she did cleaning for an old lady – before the old lady was moved into sheltered accommodation. Last of all she'd been taking *Betterware* books round the estate and doing mail order – till she got in a muddle with the paperwork and they gave it all to someone else. Now she was back on benefit while she looked for something to suit her.

She did have one job offer – and this was why Billy needed his fun. The Bricklayers' Arms pub had a bar job going, and Billy's mum suited it down to the ground. When she wore her Christmas party clothes she could sell crates of gold top to a milkman, let alone beer to thirsty bricklayers.

Billy came in from school one day and she told him about the job she'd been offered; which all sounded OK till she got to the awkward bit. She had to look the other way to tell him.

"See, Bill, it's shift work…"

"Well, you can shift. I've seen you go…"

"No, what it means is, one week in every three I've got to work till twelve at night."

"So? You don't go a-bed early."

"But I can't leave you on your own, can I?"

" 'Course you can. I'll lock the door and only tell you the password."

"No, Bill." His mum got up, lit a cigarette, put the telly on – as if the sound of it might muffle what she was about to say – "Nanny says she'll have you those weeks. You can stay there. Have your own room…"

"*Do what*?!"

"…She'll meet you from school, and take you in the mornings."

"You are having a joke?! Nanny Groaner?"

Billy couldn't believe it.

Nanny Groaner's wasn't a place for any boy. It was a grown-up's house, stuffed with things she'd bought because they got broken easily. Some things you only had to look at and they shattered, and other things were balanced on shelves just looking for a chance to jump off. Plus, Billy knew when someone liked him and when they didn't. They could smile, they could kiss, they could give you presents and put lovey-dovey words in birthday cards, but there was no getting over that look in their eye. Some teachers had it, and some didn't. Nanny Groaner wouldn't want him around for a week at a time any more than he'd want to be there. She was his dad's mother, but she did the job of a nan as if it was community service dished out by a judge – a duty, like Mrs Reynolds having to go out into the playground on Thursdays.

When Nanny Groaner was coming round to see them she always had somewhere she had to go on to – a maximum of an hour later. And it'd be in that mood that she'd look after Billy every three weeks: doing her bit for her daughter-in-law. *"No one can say I don't try…"* And Nanny Groaner doing her bit would mean

he'd live a life like some animal in a cage. An animal that went to bed early.

"You *are* joking, aren't you?"

"No, I'm not, Bill. It's a good little number they're offering me. I don't see how I can say no."

"Well, don't bother, just shake your head."

Which she did – but at him – and she went through into the kitchen and sizzled her fag in the washing-up.

"Don't you love me no more?" he shouted after her.

"Don't be stupid!" she said.

Which was a real Nanny Groaner sort of answer. Not a straight one.

Too right! He really needed fun or *something* to cheer up his life.

## CHAPTER TWO

But chasing after fun or not, the next day Billy didn't race out of the school canteen as fast as usual. It wasn't because he'd slowed up, and it wasn't because he was tempted with seconds. It was because of what Declan had found in his packed lunch. Not something to eat, and not to drink, either – there was something else, underneath the Kitkat.

It was a note from Declan's mum – a small square of paper cut from a writing pad. It said, *Mummy loves you. Be a good boy.* – and there was a small drawing of Declan's face under a little rainbow.

Declan smiled as it fluttered to the floor. "Soppy date!" he said.

Declan was a *bit* soft. He'd worn bib and braces in the Infants and even now his hair was grown long. But he was OK, he wasn't the sort who'd grass anyone up; and he could shove as hard as the rest if someone tried to get into his queue.

"What's that?" Billy asked. But he knew, and already his stomach had done a jealous head-over-heels. "You had a bust-up?"

Perhaps Declan's mum was saying sorry for something.

"No, she just… loves me." It was said very matter-of-fact, nothing to be ashamed of.

"Yeah, like *my* mum…" But after last night's news Billy definitely could have done with a little note to say so.

"Declan's had a note," Miranda Moss reported. "A lovey note – from his mum."

Billy expected a big "Woooh!", but, "Nice…" Wendy Kemp said. No one was taking the rise out of it. "I had one the other day. Goes down good with your dinner."

Billy was stuck with a bit of gristle from the mince. He swished it down with water and his mouth had a tight, sewn-up look to it. It was jealousy, definitely jealousy. When you've been shouted out of the door in the morning, all in a rush; when you haven't had time for a kiss; when you've had to remember your own reading bag and she's still in the bathroom when you call goodbye – you could do with a note to tell you she loves you. Never mind that she's got an interview at the Benefits Office, everyone's got something on. And how long does it take to write a midget note and do a couple of rainbow lines in felt-tip?

Billy thought about it. He'd always been on school dinners, his mum had never said yes to a packed lunch – not that he'd ever been bothered. But perhaps if she did, she might pick up the idea of a little note now and then. With a packed lunch there'd be something to put a message in. Perhaps if he told her about the others getting them she'd want to do it too.

But one step at a time.

"Erk! They're diabolical! Erk!" That afternoon Billy came in through the door of the flat giving it his best: the twisted face, the clutching at his throat, the going straight for the toilet making throwing-up noises.

His mum was on the phone to Nanny

Groaner. "Bill! Die a bit quieter, can't you?" But she cut the talk short and came to find him, sitting on the toilet seat trying to look white in the face. "What's up with you?"

"Them school dinners." He swallowed as if he still had that gristle in his mouth. "They need sacking, them cooks. Erk!"

"Not up to much today?"

"Not up to much? They're not up to nothing. They're like poison."

"Tell you what then, Bill, bring your dinner home tomorrow an' I'll take it down the Benefit. There's one down there I'd like to poison."

"I'm not joking!"

"Neither am I. They only reckon they're gonna stop my money!"

Billy tried to put a wild look into his eyes. "Some kids hop school sooner'n eat those dinners. Or they take packed lunches…"

That hopping-off bit worried Billy's mum – as it was meant to – but although she was young she wasn't daft. "I'll come up the school, mate, an' see what they're dishing up. Free dinners – they're supposed to give poor kids a decent meal."

"Supposed to…"

But in feeling sorry for herself over the Benefit, Billy's mum must have felt sorry for Billy, too: or his threat had worked, because she suddenly said, "I'll do you a sandwich tomorrow." And Billy nearly fell of the toilet seat in a victory spasm.

love,
mum

## CHAPTER THREE

It was a let-down, there was no disputing that. Where on earth Billy thought a proper lunchbox was coming from overnight was hard to tell – but this old plastic babywipes carton was hardly the thing to plonk on the canteen table. And the school dinner Irish stew smelled really good compared with jam sandwiches. On top of that, Declan had to have another little note, didn't he? He must have given his mum a really big kiss for yesterday's: *Who loves you, Declan? Mum does! Be good.* And there were stars all over it today instead of a rainbow. Worse, some of the others had got notes from *their* parents – there was nearly as much stuff on the table to read as there was food to eat. Suddenly, notes were as common as conkers in season. They seemed so two-a-penny that Sammy Pitt threw his in the rubbish sack. Which gave Billy his chance. He took it out, uncrumpled it and took it home in his babywipes box.

"Oh look," he said, unpacking his crusts into the bin.

"You never eat your crusts." Billy's mum was on the phone to Nanny Groaner again. "Why did God give bread crusts if you're not going to eat them?"

"It's polite to leave stuff," said Billy. "But here, look at this – a little note."

"You're too young for all that," his mum said – and went back talking to Nanny Groaner about 'the arrangements'.

The next day the rash of notes got even worse. It seemed all the packed lunch children in Billy's year had got one: big, small, handwritten, computer graphics, one on posh Barclays Bank notepaper. Only Trevor Keen didn't get one, and he pretended he'd eaten his by mistake. "Note-burger, that was!" he said – but he didn't seem to mind, he was wearing new boots which were all the rage. For Billy, though, even a Twix to go with his marmalade sandwiches couldn't make up for not

getting a little note to read.

Billy found another one thrown away and took it home.

"Here, have a look at this," he said. "Rare isn't it?"

But his mum was reciting something in her head. "St Clement's – orange juice and lemonade; Tom Collins – gin, lemon and soda water…"

"Must be quicker to write a nice little note than do the lottery, don't you reckon…?" And as a reminder he left a notepad and a Biro right next to the breadbin – she couldn't knock up a sandwich without seeing them. Except she could.

Next day there was nothing but food in his lunchbox again, while Declan's mum had done him a poem: *Who's my boy, my joy, the real McCoy – Declan! Be good. Love, Mum.*

Yuck! But wouldn't it be great to have yuck like that for dinner? Well, Billy thought, his mum just needed setting an example, that was all. So that night he left a note for her, on her pillow.

Nite-nite, sleep well, get up and give the Benefit hell.
Love, Billy
XXX.
P.S. rsvp.

(Stuff he'd learned in the Literacy Hour.)

But the next day – nothing! Except Marmite sandwiches (one half all crust) and an apple. While Declan's note went into new realms. Probably to keep a jump ahead of the rest, it was all about what a good evening they were going to have, him and his mum, going to the pictures.

And just to rub salt in his wounds, Billy was going to Nanny Groaner's for the night while his mum got shown the ropes at the pub.

# CHAPTER FOUR

Where Nanny Groaner lived wasn't a flat but a bungalow. Billy's flat was small enough but Nanny Groaner's bungalow was made even tighter by all the furniture she had in it. She used to live in a house and had gone from big to small, so it was stuffed with chairs and tables and chests and trolleys and plant stands. In the living room she had to turn sideways to get through to the kitchen, whichever route she took. And there were little pots and vases and statues everywhere – glass animals and china ladies and shepherds and bootmenders and

huntsmen and cats and monks – every flat
surface was crowded with the things
Nanny Groaner collected. There were no

premiership footballers or model racing cars, and nowhere was there a picture of Billy on a little stand, although she got given one every time the school photographer came.

Worst of all, his room wasn't *his* room, it was a spare room. Instead of a toy cupboard there was a polished wooden thing she called a tallboy, and there was no chance he could stick a band poster on the back of the door because it was hung with smelly lavender balls; while the bedside table had a knitted mat with a pink tasselly lamp on it. Cissy! *And* there was no telly in there; he'd have to watch what she watched in the sitting room – all those love stories – Nanny Groaner wouldn't want the second leg of the UEFA cup. *And* he'd be here a week at a time. How could his mum love him if she sentenced him to this?

He'd brought a few quiet things to do for

this first night, with his rucksack of pyjamas, flannel and toothbrush. Not much, because he wanted nothing with him to say he was keen on moving in...

Another thing, Nanny Groaner always called him either William or boy. Sometimes when she spoke to him he looked round to see who she was speaking to; miles different from her throwing her arms out wide and giving him a large "Billy" and a great hug, like Declan's mum would.

Even with his mum run off her feet, being at home with her was miles better than this. But she'd left him and gone off to The Bricklayers' Arms – and not so much as a *Be good!* like Declan got in his notes, but just, "Ta, Mum" to Nanny Groaner "don't take no nonsense..."

"You had your tea, boy?"

"What you got?" Billy asked. He'd decide whether or not he'd had his tea when he saw what was on offer.

"No, you've had it, haven't you?" Nanny Groaner had that all-washed-up-and-put-away look about her. Apron off, hanging on the kitchen door. She'd only asked him out of duty – as if a judge was in the cupboard listening to how kind she could

be. A chocolate biscuit or a drop of Coke wouldn't have hurt.

Billy got out some crayons and a sheet of paper; while an old magazine was straight off slid under it on the table for him to rest on.

"No fighting pictures, now – you do something nice and take your time… Then you can stay up till seven."

*Seven?* Stay up, did she call that? *Seven?* At home he hadn't got his coat off by seven. *Go down* more like – like a baby.

Well, he couldn't have this, this was desperate, this was his future life. And if this was how much he was loved between the two of them, he might as well be hated – and he'd sooner be hated at home than hated round here at Nanny Groaner's.

It was a second's decision and a micro-second's action. Scribbling a blood-red head being sliced off an alien, Billy let his arm go flying on across the paper, off the table and into a plaster statue on the sideboard: the plaster statue of a dog his mum had bought. And all at once it wasn't a plaster dog any more, it was a plaster accident, there on the carpet.

"*William!*"

That'd teach them.

But instead of being cross, Nanny Groaner was suddenly kind. Well, not kind, but *not* cross – she was more *nothing* – as if the judge was still in the cupboard.

"Your mum bought me that. You must be so sad. But accidents happen – and you're not to worry about it."

He wouldn't. But Billy tried to look sad for her, sad for his mum and sad for himself – which wasn't hard, because he *was* sad for himself. Sad because it looked like he wasn't going to get out of staying here by being a little monster.

# CHAPTER FIVE

He was taken to school next day by Nanny Groaner, who *would* insist on holding his hand. In the other one was his lunchbox, and in it some corned beef sandwiches she'd done him – and something else, because Billy had had enough of Declan and the rest showing off their lovey notes. Sitting in the canteen he rooted in his box, and from under his sandwiches he found a piece of paper.

"Would you believe it – look at this, I got one!"

No one took much notice, they were all munching and talking.

"Here, look Declan – " he persisted " – just like you."

"How, like me?"

"I got a little note."

"Oh, that."

Proudly, Billy unfolded the paper. It was about the size of half a sheet of the paper he'd been crayoning on the night before. There was a picture of a little red dog and some writing.

"I'll read it to you."

"If you've got to." But Declan was looking the other way. He'd already read his today's note and binned it.

*Dear Billy*, Billy read, *have a good day at school. Eat up all your crusts or tonite you're in for the biggest tickle I've ever give you. But you eat up the lot and we'll have a late stay-up and a bar of Froot and Nut. Lots of love, Mum.* And there were kisses all round her name, too many to count.

"Ah! Isn't that nice?" Billy asked, smoothing the paper down his front.

Declan seemed elsewhere, but Wendy Kemp had heard it.

"Cor, your mum's a lot of fun!" she said.

43

"Fun like that's better than old *love*."

"S'pose you're right," Billy agreed.

"Get her to write one for me!" Miranda Moss said.

Now Billy glowed. But Declan was chewing on something. "Who's that *from*?" he asked.

"Me mum."

"But you said your nan packed you up today. You stayed over an' she brought you to school, I saw her holding your hand."

"Yeah, well…"

"So how come your mum writ your note?"

Billy shoved the note away under a corned beef sandwich. "She must've left it with my nan to put in my lunch this morning. Just like her – being thoughtful."

"But your nan's cut your crusts off anyhow."

"Well me mum wasn't to know that."

Declan went on with his chomping and staring at Billy, so Billy finished up fast and went out to play. That was a close one! He'd nearly been sussed writing a note to himself and pretending it was from his mum.

That night he didn't have to tell her about the plaster dog, she already knew. It didn't help matters, she said, him being all arms and legs at Nan's – especially since she was probably going to have to take the pub job.

Billy cleared off to his room, didn't want to go into all that. His life was on the down – like being on the helter-skelter at the fair: up on top for a bit, then round and round

and down and down till he'd landed with a bump on the big coconut mat. But you always had to get up with a smile. You had to look as happy as the rest – and the bigger the bump, the bigger the smile had to be.

He left his next day's note there on the top of his lunchbox, the first thing to be found, nothing hidden. He'd written it on a bigger piece of paper but it was red and runny with tomato sauce coming through from his spam sandwich.

"Oh no! Not again! Another note. She's showing me up rotten!"

"Boring!" said Declan.

"Too right! Still, better see what she said."

"Better not – " said Wendy Kemp, eyeing the ketchup " – looks a bit saucy to me!"

Everyone groaned, but Billy carried on. If they had their lovey notes, he was going to have his, too.

He cleared his throat.

Dear Billy, my mate Bill,

I want to tell you how I fill.
I love you lots and like your stile,
couldn't do without your smile.
At last I've got them ends to meat
so come home quick we'll have
a treat. McDonalds.

        Lots of love,
        mum.

Declan was frowning, but some of the other faces had wide eyes and dropped-open mouths.

"Better than my note. My mum's only wrote me about the cat."

"You haven't got a cat."

"She was stuck for something to say."

"Yeah. An' mine. Nothing like Billy's."

And the eating went on with Billy sitting there in a glow of mother's love. But only made-up love, as far as he was concerned.

# CHAPTER SIX

When he got in from school his mum still looked as if she'd lost a tenner and found a pound. He put an arm round her shoulder. "Wassup, Mum? They give you a run-around last night at the pub?"

"No – but it's hard. I went wrong with the change a couple of times, and they looked at me as if I was trying to swizzle them."

"Didn't they like your top? You looked… all right… I reckoned."

"Made no odds. A full glass and the right change, that's all they're interested in. Still, beggars can't be choosers in my position. It's a job."

She went to the kitchen and shook out his babywipes box. "Didn't eat much of this, did you?"

"Wasn't hungry."

"Well, it's diabolical them serving up rough dinners. I rely on you getting a hot meal in you, dinner time."

"Yeah." But Billy was on his way to his bedroom. He felt lumpy: sort of, standing in her way. She could have gone off and had a dazzling life if it hadn't been for him. He was like a spare part – *and* he was going to have to swallow the fact that he'd be staying with Nanny Groaner for a third of his life.

And there was no doubt about it –
tomorrow would be the last packed lunch,
Billy reckoned. From what she'd said his
mum was coming to the end of her tether
with all this sandwich-making, so the last
note had to be a cracker to sign off with.

He had mixed feelings, writing it. He wouldn't be sorry to be off old bread and scrape and back onto something hot and tasty – that was one feeling. But mixed with it was a sad feeling at what he was writing in his forged note, because he was wishing it was his mum who'd put pen to paper, like the other mums.

But that day there weren't many others with notes to show. Somehow, Billy's note of yesterday had topped the lot, and even if some of the others had got them, they weren't being waved about and read to everyone.

Declan was wearing a badge instead – *Mum loves Declan* – but he didn't bother pointing to it, even.

Anyway, this was going to be the last so Billy made the best of it.

"No – I don't believe it!" He pulled his last piece of writing-paper out from under a fishpaste sandwich. "Another show-up! Oh no, I'm too embarrassed to read this out."

"Don't then," said Declan.

"What she's written. It's so yucky!"

"Leave it, then."

"No – I mean, listen to this."

Declan found time that moment to go

to the waste bin, but Wendy Kemp and Miranda Moss were all ears.

"Is it like yesterday's?"

"Go on – you read it, Billy."

Billy tried to look reluctant, but when Wendy Kemp started to move away he got reading fast.

Dear Billy,

I've had a mad idea. What about you and me book up for Disneyland, the one in Parris? We'll get down the travel shop tonite. And go at half term. Yeah? Be good, won't it?

Lots of love, forever and always, Mum. x x x x x

"Aaaah…" said Billy. He felt choked himself, reading it – even though he was the writer.

"That's beautiful," said Wendy Kemp. You want to frame that."

"You want to burn it! I never wrote that stuff! *Disneyland*?! I can't afford to shop in *Iceland*."

Billy spun round so fast his head nearly swivelled off and fell into his babywipes box. While he'd been reading out loud, someone had come up to stand behind him. His mum.

"Mum!"

"Bill! You little twicer! *Who* are you saying's signed that?"

Billy choked on fishpaste from eight mouthfuls back. "No one," he said. "I was having a laugh…"

"Ha blooming ha."

"What you doing here?" His heart would

take till Thursday to get over the jumping it had done.

"Came up to complain about the poison meals." She looked round the canteen. "Chicken nuggets and chips, jelly and ice cream – I had a taste, it don't seem like poison to me."

"Yeah, well..." Billy tried another bite of fishpaste but his mouth wasn't having any. He looked here, looked there, and looked back at his mum. There was something funny about her, too, something different –

something she was wearing. "What are you doing in that dinner lady's stuff?"

"Came in to complain about the dinners, and guess who Cook is? Mrs Taylor, used to run the greengrocer's where I worked. She's one short today so she let me stay, soon as I gave her dinners the thumbs-up."

"Oh." Life was too complicated sometimes.

"And guess what?" Her face was pretty with its smile, like a little girl with a new present. "I'm filling in for a woman on holiday, all next week, who's probably leaving. And when they've checked up on me, and if I suit, there's a good chance I can stay on."

"Yeah!" Billy punched the air. "So you won't have to..." He nodded in the direction of where he reckoned The Bricklayers' Arms was.

"No. Good, eh?"

"And I won't have to…" He nodded the opposite way, in the Nanny Groaner direction.

"That's right. It'll be less money, but the school dates'll be great for us both – and I won't have to lose you for a week at a time."

Billy swallowed and looked into her eyes. What had she said? From behind him he could feel Declan looking too. And Wendy Kemp. And Miranda Moss. And Trevor Keen.

"Why, would you miss me at Nanny Groaner's?"

"Miss you? I cried myself to sleep the other night!"

Billy would have swallowed again if he'd had anything left to swallow. "I thought you didn't mind me going."

"Mind? 'Course I mind. It breaks me up, the thought of it. I love you too much not

to mind." Lovely and loud, she said it, for everyone to hear.

"Aaaaah," said Wendy Kemp.

"Oooooh," said Miranda Moss.

"Eeeeee!" said Declan, but he was pretending to be sick. Jealous sick.

"Stupid Bill!" She ruffled Billy's hair, then she stood up straight like a real dinner

lady and pulled her official overall tight.
"Now then, young man," she said, "you can
eat up them crusts or you won't get no tea
tonight."

And, pulling a moany face to cover his
joyful feeling inside, Billy ate every bit of
his sandwiches and buried the babywipes
box deep in the bin.

# Order Form

To order direct from the publishers, just make a list of the titles you want and fill in the form below:

Name ..............................................................................................

Address ..........................................................................................

.......................................................................................................

.......................................................................................................

Send to: Dept 6, HarperCollins Publishers Ltd, Westerhill Road, Bishopbriggs, Glasgow G64 2QT.

Please enclose a cheque or postal order to the value of the cover price, plus:

UK & BFPO: Add £1.00 for the first book, and 25p per copy for each additional book ordered.

Overseas and Eire: Add £2.95 service charge. Books will be sent by surface mail but quotes for airmail despatch will be given on request.

A 24-hour telephone ordering service is available to holders of Visa, MasterCard, Amex or Switch cards on 0141- 772 2281.

Collins
An *Imprint* of HarperCollins*Publishers*